Associated Board Brass Scales and Arpeggios

Series Editors **John Wallace** and **Ian Denley**

Scales and Arpeggios for Horn

Grades 1-8

It is often maintained, with some justification, that brass-players frequently show reluctance to learn scales and arpeggios thoroughly. The horn has an enormous range and the study of scales and arpeggios is essential for achieving this range. Scales and arpeggios also make very useful exercises for developing an embouchure which adjusts smoothly without any 'breaks' from the very high right through to the very low.

Committed and assiduous practice of scales and arpeggios also assists greatly in developing a fluent technique and the transposition skills so necessary on the horn.

This manual seeks to assist this situation by including a comprehensive chart of recommended fingerings and a useful table of harmonics, together with hints on problems to avoid and useful advice appended to the scales and arpeggios most likely to be problematic. The aim is to help students learn their scales and arpeggios thoroughly, as well as provide support material for those brass teachers who may not be specialists on the horn.

We are most grateful to Phillip Eastop, Professor of Horn at the Royal Academy of Music, and Robin Tait, Head of Performing Arts at Bridlington School, for acting as specialist advisers for this manual.

JOHN WALLACE and IAN DENLEY   1995

**The Associated Board of
the Royal Schools of Music**

Fingering chart

This comprehensive fingering chart and guides in this manual apply to the modern double horn in B♭/F. The shaded fingerings are those recommended for use within the Associated Board's scales and arpeggios (see p.4). As well as giving the fingerings necessary to cover the Associated Board's requirements, the chart also includes useful additional fingerings at either end of the horn's compass, for notes found in some advanced repertoire.

Chart 1 (bass clef)

	C	C#	D	Eb	E	F	F#	G	G#	A	Bb	B	C	C#	D	Eb	E	F	F#	G
F HORN	O						1 2 3	1 3	2 3	**1 2**	**1**	2	**O**	1 2 3	1 3	2 3	1 2	1	**2**	**O**
B♭ HORN		2 3	1 2	1	2	O						1 2 3	1 3	**2 3**	**1 2**	**1**	**2**	**O**	**1 2 3**	**1 3**

Chart 2 (treble clef)

	G#	A	Bb	B	C	C#	D	Eb	E	F	F#	G	G#	A	Bb	B	C
F HORN	2 3	1 2	1	2	O	1 2	1	2 3	O	1	2	**O**	2 3	1 2	1	2	O
B♭ HORN	**2 3**	**1 2**	**1**	**2**	**O**	**2 3**	**1 2**	**1**	**2**	**O**	**1 2**	**1 3**	**1***	**2 3**	**1 2**	**1**	**2**	**O**

* This fingering for G² tends to be slightly flat on the B♭ side, but it is very useful in quick runs because it avoids the use of the 3rd valve and thumb valve which always feel slightly more cumbersome than the 1st and 2nd valves when playing at speed.

Chart 3 (treble clef)

	C#	D	Eb	E	F	F#	G	G#	A	Bb	B	C	C#	D
F HORN	1 2	2	O	2	O	1	O	2 3	1 2	1	2	O		
B♭ HORN	**2 3**	**1 2**	**1**	**2**	**O**	**1 2**	**O**	**2 3**	**1 2**	**1**	**2**	**O**	**2 3**	**1 2**

Key to symbols

1	LH index finger	3	LH ring finger	LH	left hand
2	LH middle finger	O	all fingers off	RH	right hand

The fourth valve, operated by the LH thumb, is the one which changes the 'side' of the instrument from F to B♭ (see p.5).

Tables of harmonics

As a source for the exploration of alternative fingerings, the following tables illustrate the notes available from each combination of valves (i.e. each length of tubing). This is known as the *harmonic series*. The first note in each row is the *fundamental* or *pedal note*. The numbered notes which follow the fundamental, obtainable from each valve combination by embouchure adjustment, are known as *harmonics*, or *upper partials*.

The fundamental note is only occasionally used; fundamental notes in brackets are virtually impossible to obtain. Within the upper partials, notes in brackets do not fit into any modern western scales and so should be reserved for specialized pitch requirements.

Strictly speaking, there is no upper limit to the harmonic series, but it must be stressed that these extremes of range depend greatly on the correct development of the embouchure muscles and should be approached with care.

B♭ Fingering

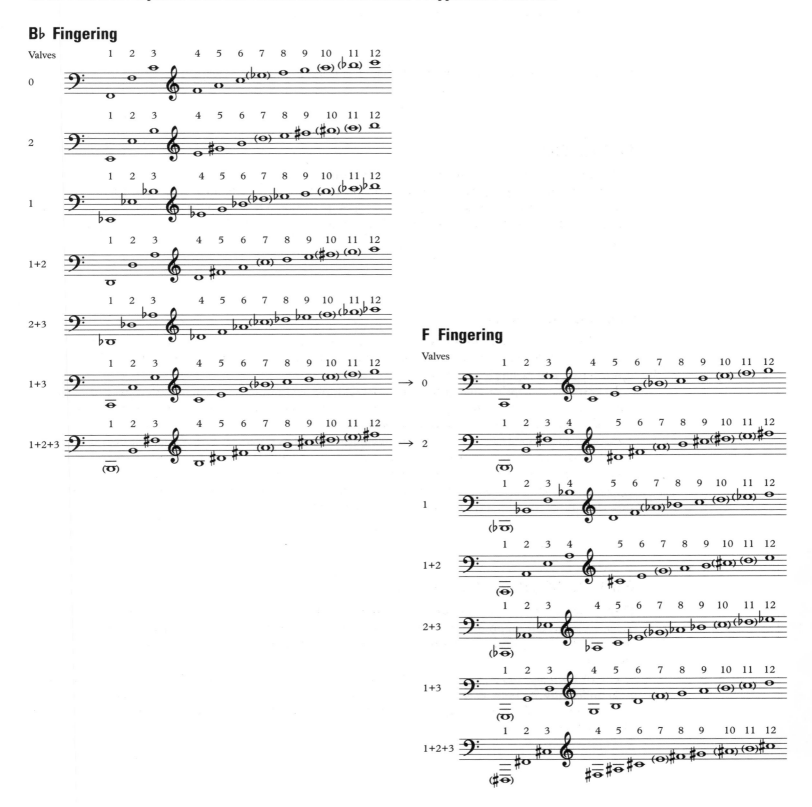

F Fingering

Guide to fingering

For reference purposes, where notes are indicated throughout the manual with a small superscript number (e.g. Bb^1, E^2, $F\#^3$, etc.), this refers to their position within the horn's range:

A^1 ——— $G\#^1$ A^2 ——— $G\#^2$ A^3 ——— $G\#^3$ A^4 ——— B^4

The range of notes within the Associated Board's scales and arpeggios is from A^1 to B^4.

The Bass Clef

In this manual the bass clef is used in those scales and arpeggios which descend below C^1. This serves to avoid too many ledger lines and reinforces the fact that this clef is a familiar sight in much horn repertoire, especially the orchestral repertoire. It should be noted that so-called 'modern' notation is used, that is, as with the treble clef, notes printed in the bass clef must be read so that they sound a perfect 5th lower.

Fingering Differences

For clarity, the fingering chart treats the two sides of the horn separately. In practice, however, it is essential to feel the instrument to be an integrated whole and to use the fourth valve (the Bb/F valve) with as much ease and facility as the other three.

All horns have slightly different idiosyncrasies with regard to tuning. The fingerings suggested in the chart have been chosen for their general reliability on most modern instruments. For some notes there are many alternative fingerings possible; these can be seen on the Table of harmonics on p.3.

Players using a single Bb instrument are obviously limited to the lower row of fingerings in the chart. However, as most such horns have a valve either for 'F extension' or for hand-stopping, or both, it is possible to get most if not all of the missing notes by a makeshift combination of using a fingering which will get near to the note, whilst at the same time bending it the rest of the way down with the lips. The difficulty of this technique should not be underestimated.

Tonal and Articulation Considerations

There is general agreement amongst horn-players that the Bb side is the best one to use for the upper register. Conversely, to produce the highest quality timbre in slow, sonorous passages in the middle and lower register, it is generally better to play on the F side, although there is some loss of clarity in articulation.

The Bb horn also makes articulation from one note to the next much easier. As clear articulation and tonal uniformity are both essential in scales and arpeggios, the shaded fingerings in the chart are recommended for the Associated Board's requirements as they make good use of the advantages of both F and Bb sides of the horn.

Mechanical Differences

Some horns stand in B♭ until the fourth valve is depressed, accessing the longer tubes of the F side of the instrument. Other horns stand in F with the fourth valve switching back to the shorter tubing of the B♭ side. Most horns can be set up either way and both ways work well. However, in the early stages of learning, it is recommended that if possible the fourth valve be adjusted so that the instrument stands in B♭. This will facilitate later use, if required, of an instrument with *two* thumb valves, the extra valve most likely compensating for the pitch shift caused by muting the horn with the tightly cupped RH – a traditional and much-used technique known as 'hand-stopping'.

Enharmonic note-names

Two or three notes having the same sound but different names are called *enharmonics*; for example, E♭ is the enharmonic of D♯. A full table is given below to guide students in the fingering of those notes in certain scales and arpeggios which may be unfamiliarly notated.

C	=	B♯	=	D♭♭		E	=	F♭	=	D𝄪		G♯	=	A♭
C♯	=	D♭	=	B𝄪		F	=	E♯	=	G♭♭		A	=	G𝄪	=	B♭♭
D	=	C𝄪	=	E♭♭		F♯	=	G♭	=	E𝄪		B♭	=	A♯	=	C♭♭
E♭	=	D♯	=	F♭♭		G	=	F𝄪	=	A♭♭		B	=	C♭	=	A𝄪

Notes on the requirements

Reference must always be made to the syllabus for the year in which the examination is to be taken, in case any changes have been made to the requirements.

In the examination all scales and arpeggios must be played from memory.

Candidates should aim to play their scales and arpeggios at a pace that allows accuracy, with a uniform tone across all registers and a rhythmic flow without undue accentuation, as well as with even tonguing and good intonation. Recommended speeds are given on p.7.

In Grades 1-5 candidates may choose *either* the melodic *or* the harmonic form of the minor scale; in Grades 6-8 candidates are required to play *both* forms.

The choice of breathing place is left to the candidate's discretion, but taking a breath must not be allowed to disturb the flow of the scale or arpeggio. If a breath is taken during the course of a slurred scale or arpeggio, a *soft* tongue attack should be made on the note following the breath.

It is desirable that students do not use a breath as a means of disguising an embouchure 'break', where the position of the lips on the mouthpiece has to be re-seated as the player moves from one register to another in the course of a scale or arpeggio. Whilst embouchure breaks are quite common, it is preferable to be free from them as they do cause difficulties and can be avoided.

Articulation

It is very important for the foundation of good articulation that players use the *tongue* to articulate, rather than just the breath, which is a common error at the elementary level. The sound must be well-supported by diaphragmatic breathing throughout all forms of articulation, so that the tone does not deteriorate (usually with attendant intonation problems), especially when tonguing *staccato*.

Four different forms of articulation are found in the scale and arpeggio requirements: slurred, tongued, *legato*-tongued and *staccato*. In Grades 1-6 candidates are required to play scales and arpeggios both slurred and tongued; in Grades 7 and 8 candidates are required to play scales and arpeggios slurred, *legato*-tongued and *staccato*.

In slurred scales and arpeggios there is no gap between the notes, whereas the gap is large when playing *staccato*. In *legato*-tonguing the effect is almost slurred, but there is the smallest separation achieved by a very soft tongue attack.

The articulations may be visualized like this:

slurred ——————————————————————

tongued ——   ——   ——   ——

legato-tongued ———   ———   ———   ———

staccato –   –   –   –

Legato-tonguing is often considered by brass players to be a fusion of *tenuto* and *legato*; it is sometimes described as 'soft'-tonguing or as an 'articulated slur'. Perhaps the least familiar of the articulation forms required, it may usefully be notated as follows:

Current requirements for Grades 1-8

This table lists scales and arpeggios required for each grade; numbers refer to those printed alongside the scales and arpeggios in the following pages.

Grade 1   1, 49 *or* 50, 82, 117

Grade 2   1, 16, 29 *or* 30, 65 *or* 66, 82, 97, 107, 125

Grade 3   9, 12, 23 *or* 24, 35, *or* 36, 43 *or* 44, 73, 90, 93, 104, 110, 114

Grade 4   6, 7, 17, 39 *or* 40, 51 *or* 52, 67 *or* 68, 78, 87, 88, 98, 112, 118, 126, 129

Grade 5   4, 5, 10, 17, 31 *or* 32, 37 *or* 38, 41 *or* 42, 75, 85, 86, 91, 98, 108, 111, 113, 130

Grade 6   2, 3, 8, 11, 27, 28, 33, 34, 45, 46, 55, 56, 74, 75, 76, 77, 83, 84, 89, 92, 106, 109, 115, 120, 132, 143

Grade 7   2, 3, 4, 5, 6, 7, 8, 10, 11, 13, 14, 18, 19, 21, 25, 26, 27, 28, 31, 32, 33, 34, 37, 38, 39, 40, 41, 42, 45, 46, 47, 48, 53, 54, 55, 56, 59, 60, 61, 62, 69, 70, (Chromatic scale requirements: see note to No.79), 83, 84, 85, 86, 87, 88, 89, 91, 92, 94, 95, 99, 100, 102, 105, 106, 108, 109, 111, 112, 113, 115, 116, 119, 120, 122, 123, 127, 130, 131, 132, 141, 142, 144

Grade 8   2, 3, 4, 5, 6, 7, 8, 10, 11, 15, 20, 22, 25, 26, 27, 28, 31, 32, 33, 34, 37, 38, 39, 40, 41, 42, 45, 46, 47, 48, 57, 58, 63, 64, 71, 72, (Chromatic scale requirements: see note to No.79), 80, 81, 83, 84, 85, 86, 87, 88, 89, 91, 92, 96, 101, 103, 105, 106, 108, 109, 111, 112, 113, 115, 116, 121, 124, 128, 130, 131, 132, 133, 134, 135, 136, 137, 138, 139, 140, 141, 143, 144, 145

Recommended speeds

The following recommended *minimum* speeds are given as a general guide. It is essential that scales and arpeggios are played at a speed rapid enough to allow well-organized breathing, yet steady enough to allow a well-focused sound with good intonation across the range.

major and minor scales, chromatic scales, whole-tone scales, dominant and diminished sevenths			*major and minor arpeggios*		
Grade 1	♩ =	50	♪ =	72
Grade 2	♩ =	56	♪ =	80
Grade 3	♩ =	66	♪ =	92
Grade 4	♩ =	72	♪ =	100
Grade 5	♩ =	80	♪ =	112
Grade 6	♩ =	96	♩. =	56
Grade 7	♩ =	108	♩. =	66
Grade 8	♩ =	120	♩. =	76

ordered 10/12 from www.wilko.com
eda 29/12
01284 725 725
ref 275 25 86

Ronald Hanner
Suite for Horn.
Emerson

list C

Major Scales

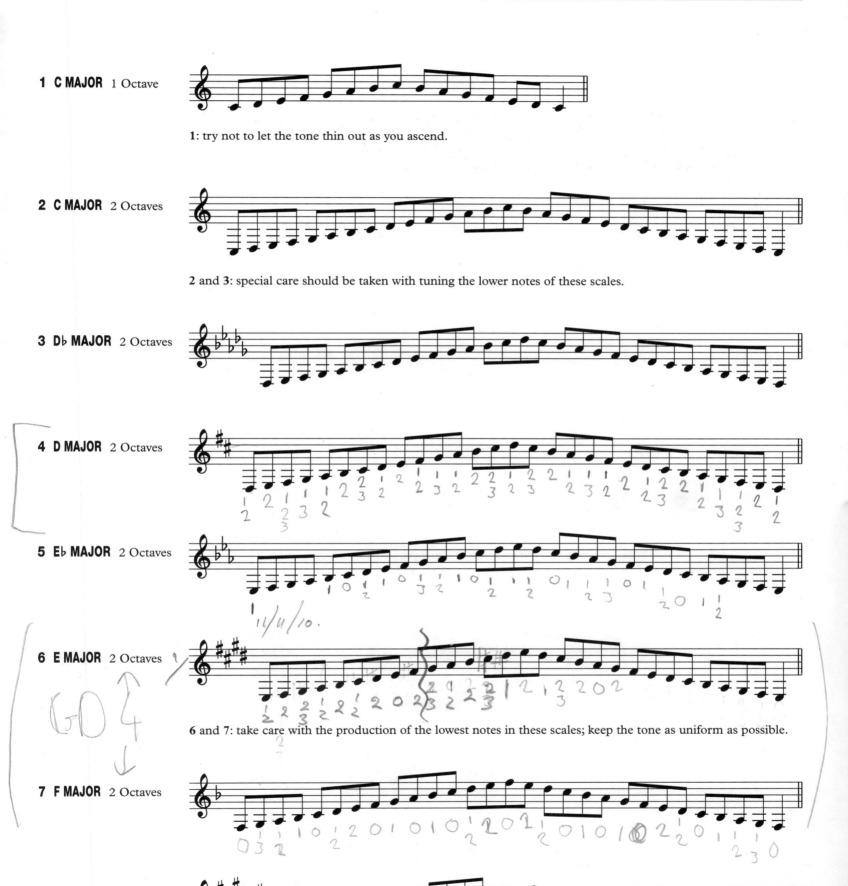

1 C MAJOR 1 Octave

1: try not to let the tone thin out as you ascend.

2 C MAJOR 2 Octaves

2 and 3: special care should be taken with tuning the lower notes of these scales.

3 Db MAJOR 2 Octaves

4 D MAJOR 2 Octaves

5 Eb MAJOR 2 Octaves

6 E MAJOR 2 Octaves

6 and 7: take care with the production of the lowest notes in these scales; keep the tone as uniform as possible.

7 F MAJOR 2 Octaves

8 F# MAJOR 2 Octaves

9 G MAJOR A Twelfth

9: if using the F horn for G¹ (low G), take special care in co-ordinating the thumb-valve and 1 & 2 for A.

10 G MAJOR 2 Octaves

11 Ab MAJOR 2 Octaves

12 A MAJOR A Twelfth

12: keep focused tone during the top four notes of this scale.

13 A MAJOR 2 Octaves (Lower)

13: aim for real clarity of attack in the production of the extreme low notes.

14 A MAJOR 2 Octaves (Upper)

15 A MAJOR 3 Octaves

15: this and all other 3-octave scales combine all the technical and tonal complexity so far encountered. Special care must be taken to preserve uniformity of tone and intonation across the range.

16 **B♭ MAJOR** 1 Octave

16: take care with the co-ordination of the fingers if using 1 & 3 on the
B♭ side for G.

17 **B♭ MAJOR** A Twelfth

18 **B♭ MAJOR** 2 Octaves
(Lower)

18: aim for real clarity of attack in the production of the extreme low notes.

19 **B♭ MAJOR** 2 Octaves
(Upper)

19: control of the air flow and careful training of the embouchure are the key to producing the highest notes of
this scale successfully. Focusing on the *slurred* version initially will assist the process.

20 **B♭ MAJOR** 3 Octaves

20: this and all other 3-octave scales combine all the technical and tonal complexity so far encountered. Special
care must be taken to preserve uniformity of tone and intonation across the range.

21 **B MAJOR** 2 Octaves

21: aim for real clarity of attack in the production of the extreme low notes.

22 **B MAJOR** 3 Octaves

22: this and all other 3-octave scales combine all the technical and tonal complexity so far encountered. Special
care must be taken to preserve uniformity of tone and intonation across the range.

Minor Scales

23 C MINOR melodic
1 Octave

23 and 24: take care with the co-ordination of the fingers if using 1 & 3 on the B♭ side for G.

24 C MINOR harmonic
1 Octave

25 C MINOR melodic
2 Octaves

26 C MINOR harmonic
2 Octaves

27 C♯ MINOR melodic
2 Octaves

27 and 28: special care should be taken with tuning the lower notes of these scales.

28 C♯ MINOR harmonic
2 Octaves

29 D MINOR melodic
1 Octave

29: take care with the finger co-ordination at the top of this scale.

30 D MINOR harmonic
1 Octave

30: B♭ to C♯ needs careful negotiation. Take care with the finger co-ordination at the top of this scale.

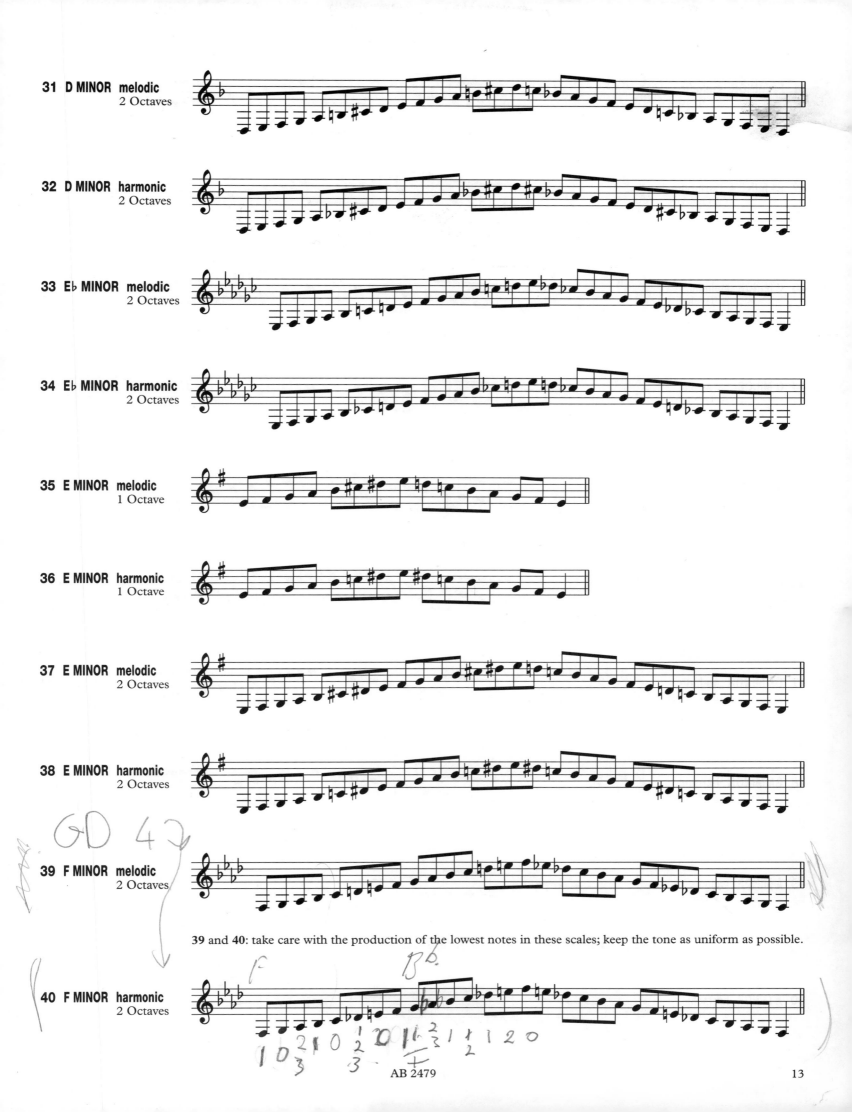

31 D MINOR melodic
2 Octaves

32 D MINOR harmonic
2 Octaves

33 E♭ MINOR melodic
2 Octaves

34 E♭ MINOR harmonic
2 Octaves

35 E MINOR melodic
1 Octave

36 E MINOR harmonic
1 Octave

37 E MINOR melodic
2 Octaves

38 E MINOR harmonic
2 Octaves

39 F MINOR melodic
2 Octaves

39 and **40**: take care with the production of the lowest notes in these scales; keep the tone as uniform as possible.

40 F MINOR harmonic
2 Octaves

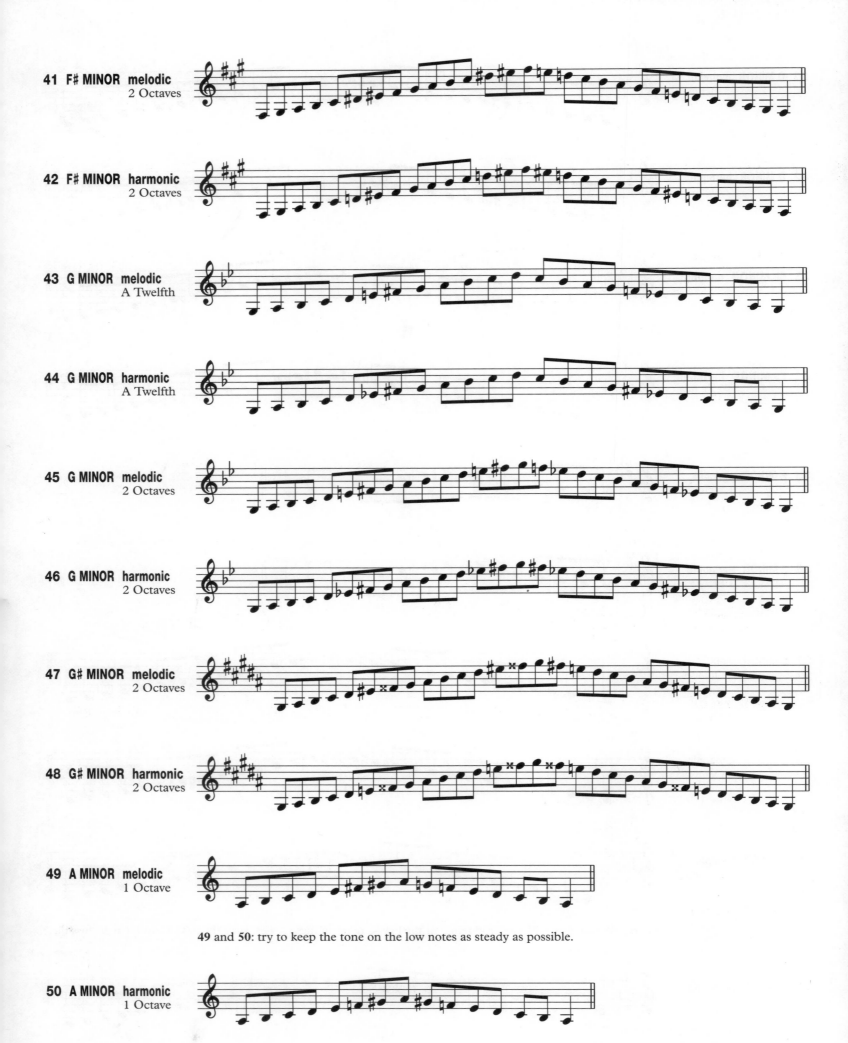

41 F# MINOR melodic
2 Octaves

42 F# MINOR harmonic
2 Octaves

43 G MINOR melodic
A Twelfth

44 G MINOR harmonic
A Twelfth

45 G MINOR melodic
2 Octaves

46 G MINOR harmonic
2 Octaves

47 G# MINOR melodic
2 Octaves

48 G# MINOR harmonic
2 Octaves

49 A MINOR melodic
1 Octave

49 and **50**: try to keep the tone on the low notes as steady as possible.

50 A MINOR harmonic
1 Octave

51 A MINOR melodic
A Twelfth

52 A MINOR harmonic
A Twelfth

53 A MINOR melodic
2 Octaves (Lower)

53 and **54:** aim for real clarity of attack in the production of the extreme low notes.

54 A MINOR harmonic
2 Octaves (Lower)

55 A MINOR melodic
2 Octaves (Upper)

55 and **56:** control of the air flow and careful training of the embouchure are the key to producing the highest notes of these scales successfully. Focusing on the *slurred* version initially will assist the process.

56 A MINOR harmonic
2 Octaves (Upper)

57 A MINOR melodic
3 Octaves

57 and **58:** these scales combine all the technical and tonal complexity so far encountered. Special care must be taken to preserve uniformity of tone and intonation across the range.

58 A MINOR harmonic
3 Octaves

59 B♭ MINOR melodic
2 Octaves (Lower)

59 and **60**: aim for real clarity of attack in the production of the extreme low notes.

60 B♭ MINOR harmonic
2 Octaves (Lower)

61 B♭ MINOR melodic
2 Octaves (Upper)

62 B♭ MINOR harmonic
2 Octaves (Upper)

63 B♭ MINOR melodic
3 Octaves

63 and **64**: special care must be taken to preserve uniformity of tone and intonation across the range.

64 B♭ MINOR harmonic
3 Octaves

65 B MINOR melodic
1 Octave

65 and **66**: using 1 on the B♭ side for G will help to avoid co-ordination problems with the fingering.

66 B MINOR harmonic
1 Octave

67 B MINOR melodic
A Twelfth

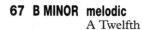

67 and 68: the lip tension needs to be carefully calculated between top E and F♯ and back, especially when slurred.

68 B MINOR harmonic
A Twelfth

69 B MINOR melodic
2 Octaves

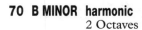

69 and 70: aim for real clarity of attack in the production of the extreme low notes.

70 B MINOR harmonic
2 Octaves

71 B MINOR melodic
3 Octaves

71 and 72: special care must be taken to preserve uniformity of tone and intonation across the range.

72 B MINOR harmonic
3 Octaves

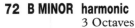

Chromatic Scales

73 on C 1 Octave

73: take special care with finger co-ordination, especially when slurred.

74 on E 2 Octaves

75 on F 2 Octaves

75: take special care to grade the lip tension across the whole range.

76 on F# 2 Octaves

77 on G 2 Octaves

78 on A A Twelfth

79 from C¹ to B⁴

79: control of the air flow and careful training of the embouchure are the key to producing the highest notes of this scale successfully. Focusing on the *slurred* version initially will assist the process.

The chromatic scale requirements for Grades 7 and 8 can be taken from No.79 above.

Grades 7 and **8**   On any note – two octaves

Whole-Tone Scales

80 on C 2 Octaves

81 on B 2 Octaves

Major Arpeggios

82 C MAJOR 1 Octave

82: take care to negotiate G² to C³ and back really precisely, especially when slurred.

83 C MAJOR 2 Octaves

83 and **84**: special care should be taken with tuning the lower notes of these arpeggios.

84 D♭ MAJOR 2 Octaves

85 D MAJOR 2 Octaves

86 E♭ MAJOR 2 Octaves

87 E MAJOR 2 Octaves

87 and **88**: try to preserve tonal uniformity throughout.

88 F MAJOR 2 Octaves

AB 2479

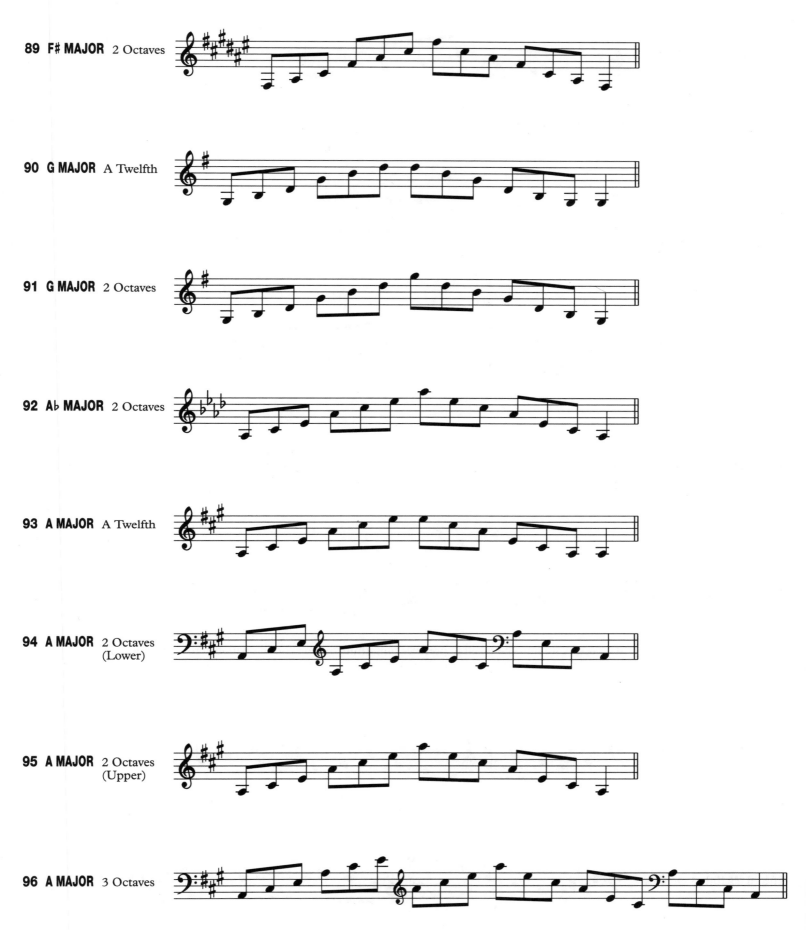

89 F♯ MAJOR 2 Octaves

90 G MAJOR A Twelfth

91 G MAJOR 2 Octaves

92 A♭ MAJOR 2 Octaves

93 A MAJOR A Twelfth

94 A MAJOR 2 Octaves (Lower)

95 A MAJOR 2 Octaves (Upper)

96 A MAJOR 3 Octaves

96: special care must be taken to preserve uniformity of tone and intonation across the range. Try not to let the sound tighten in the upper reaches—keep it full.

97 B♭ MAJOR 1 Octave

97: take care to negotiate F² to B♭³ and back really precisely, especially when slurred.

98 B♭ MAJOR A Twelfth

99 B♭ MAJOR 2 Octaves (Lower)

100 B♭ MAJOR 2 Octaves (Upper)

101 B♭ MAJOR 3 Octaves

101: special care must be taken to preserve uniformity of tone and intonation across the range. Try not to let the sound tighten in the upper reaches—keep it full.

102 B MAJOR 2 Octaves

103 B MAJOR 3 Octaves

103: special care must be taken to preserve uniformity of tone and intonation across the range. Try not to let the sound tighten in the upper reaches—keep it full.

Minor Arpeggios

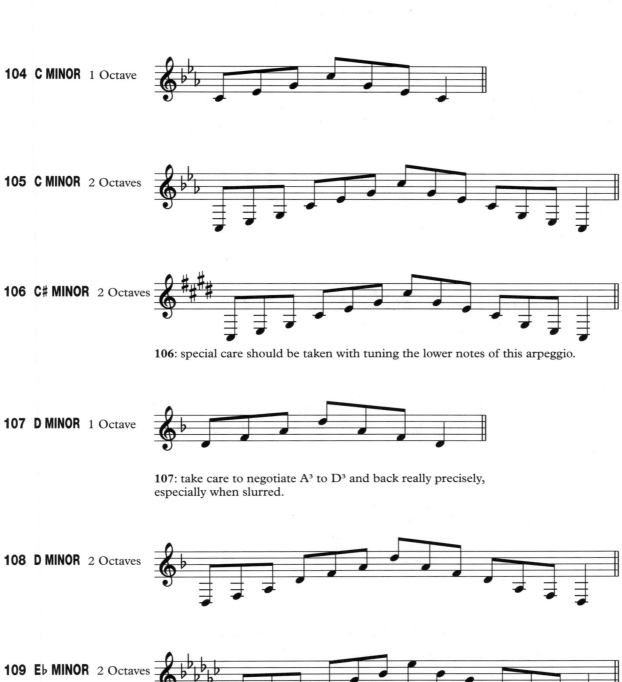

104 C MINOR 1 Octave

105 C MINOR 2 Octaves

106 C# MINOR 2 Octaves

106: special care should be taken with tuning the lower notes of this arpeggio.

107 D MINOR 1 Octave

107: take care to negotiate A^3 to D^3 and back really precisely, especially when slurred.

108 D MINOR 2 Octaves

109 E♭ MINOR 2 Octaves

110 E MINOR 1 Octave

111 E MINOR 2 Octaves

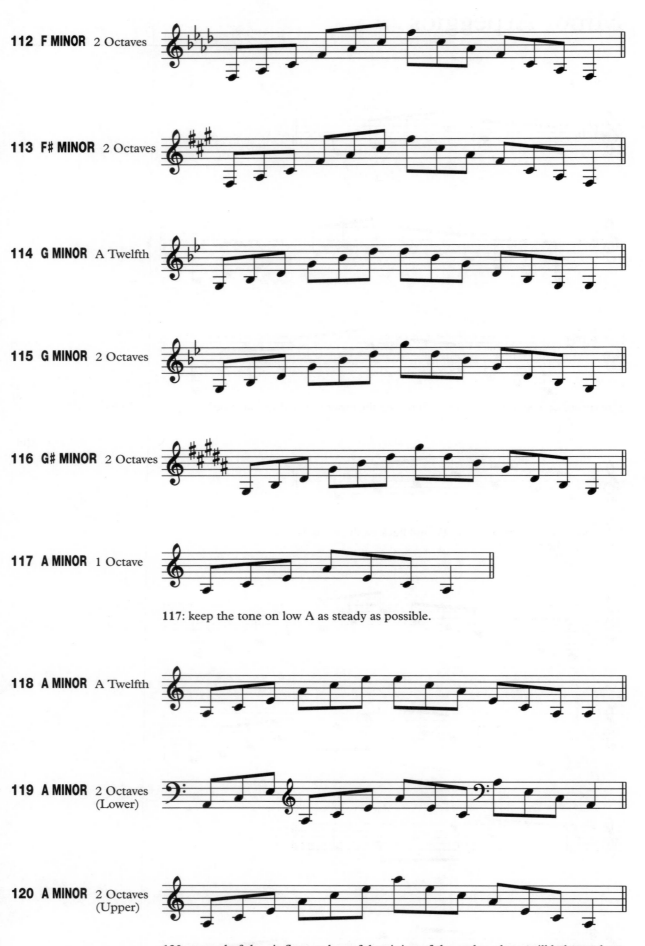

112 F MINOR 2 Octaves

113 F# MINOR 2 Octaves

114 G MINOR A Twelfth

115 G MINOR 2 Octaves

116 G# MINOR 2 Octaves

117 A MINOR 1 Octave

117: keep the tone on low A as steady as possible.

118 A MINOR A Twelfth

119 A MINOR 2 Octaves (Lower)

120 A MINOR 2 Octaves (Upper)

120: control of the air flow and careful training of the embouchure will help produce A^4 (top A) successfully.

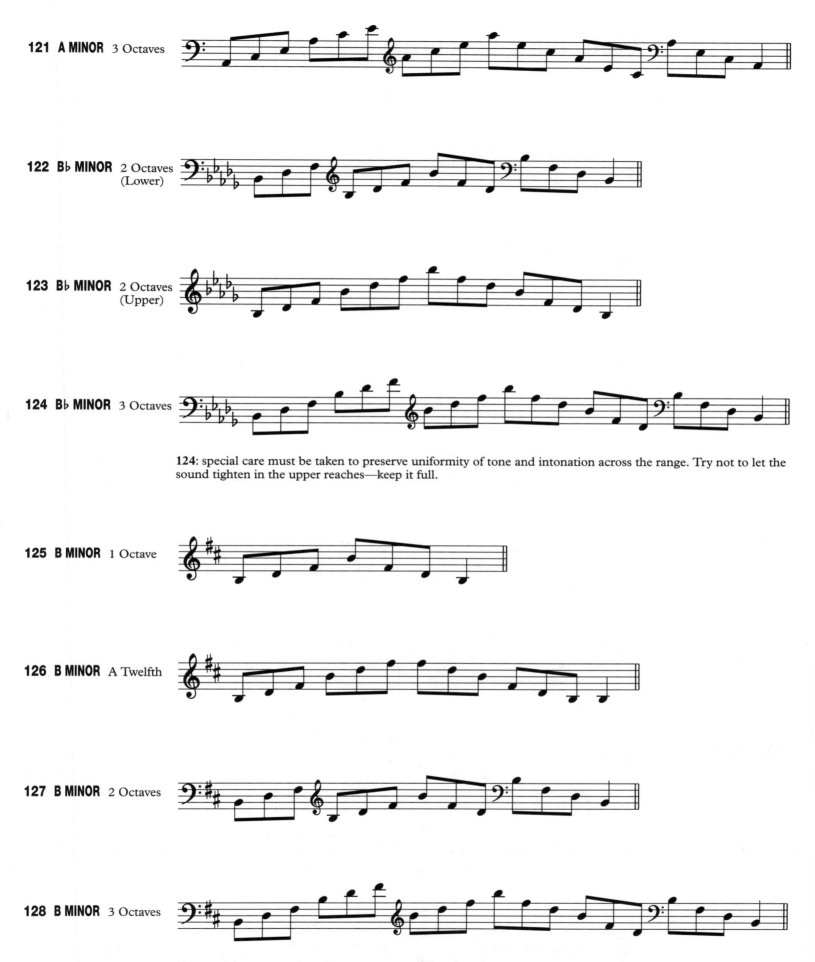

121 A MINOR 3 Octaves

122 Bb MINOR 2 Octaves (Lower)

123 Bb MINOR 2 Octaves (Upper)

124 Bb MINOR 3 Octaves

124: special care must be taken to preserve uniformity of tone and intonation across the range. Try not to let the sound tighten in the upper reaches—keep it full.

125 B MINOR 1 Octave

126 B MINOR A Twelfth

127 B MINOR 2 Octaves

128 B MINOR 3 Octaves

128: special care must be taken to preserve uniformity of tone and intonation across the range. Try not to let the sound tighten in the upper reaches—keep it full.

Dominant Sevenths

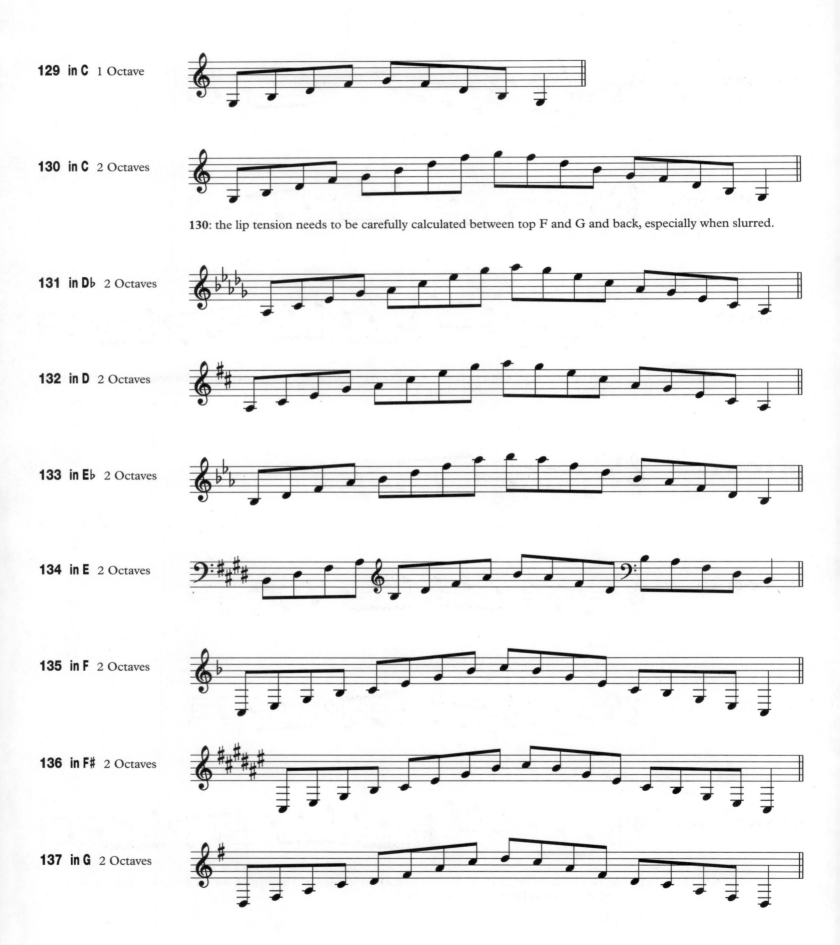

129 in C 1 Octave

130 in C 2 Octaves

130: the lip tension needs to be carefully calculated between top F and G and back, especially when slurred.

131 in D♭ 2 Octaves

132 in D 2 Octaves

133 in E♭ 2 Octaves

134 in E 2 Octaves

135 in F 2 Octaves

136 in F♯ 2 Octaves

137 in G 2 Octaves

138 in Ab 2 Octaves

139 in A 2 Octaves

140 in Bb 2 Octaves

141 in B 2 Octaves

Diminished Sevenths

142 on C 2 Octaves

143 on G 2 Octaves

144 on Ab 2 Octaves

145 on A 2 Octaves

Music and text origination by
Barnes Music Engraving Ltd, East Sussex
Printed in England by Caligraving Ltd, Thetford, Norfolk

3.10